Lost but found

A Boy's Story of Grief and Recovery

Written by Lauren Persons
with illustrations by Noah Hrbek

Loving Healing Press
Ann Arbor, MI

Lost But Found: A Boy's Story of Grief and Recovery
Copyright © 2021 by Lauren Persons. All Rights Reserved.

Illustrations by Noah Hrbek

Library of Congress Cataloging-in-Publication Data

Names: Persons, Lauren, 1953- author. | Hrbek, Noah, illustrator.
Title: Lost but found : a boy's story of grief and recovery / written by Lauren Persons ; with illustrations by Noah Hrbek.
Description: Ann Arbor, MI : Loving Healing Press, [2021] | Audience: Ages 4-6 years. | Audience: Grades K-1. | Summary: "Based on the author's experience of trying to explain to a 3-year-old boy that his father was not coming home from the hospital, this book explores the confusion that a young child experiences around bereavement. Ultimately, the boy discovers his father lives on within his heart"-- Provided by publisher.

Identifiers: LCCN 2020050721 (print) | LCCN 2020050722 (ebook) | ISBN 9781615995479 (paperback) | ISBN 9781615995486 (hardcover) | ISBN 9781615995493 (kindle edition) | ISBN 9781615995493 (epub)
Subjects: CYAC: Death--Fiction. | Fathers and sons--Fiction.
Classification: LCC PZ7.1.P44775 Los 2021 (print) | LCC PZ7.1.P44775 (ebook) | DDC [E]--dc23
LC record available at https://lccn.loc.gov/2020050721
LC ebook record available at https://lccn.loc.gov/2020050722

Published by
Loving Healing Press
5145 Pontiac Trail
Ann Arbor, MI 48105

www.LHPress.com
info@LHPress.com

Phone 888-761-6268
FAX 734-663-6861

Distributed by
Ingram (USA/CAN/AU), Betram's Books (UK/EU)

Author's Note:

One of the hardest things I have ever had to do in my life is to explain to my young son what happened to his father. How do you tell your three-year-old that his daddy won't be home from the hospital this time? It never failed, when I thought he finally understood his father was dead, he would ask me, "So, is Daddy coming home tomorrow?" The reality was that this was just hard stuff to understand. Why wasn't his dad coming home? Why was my husband not going to share our lives? I still don't know exactly. I wrote this book to let the elephant in the room run amok, to allow children to ask questions, and talk about their fears and feelings. What I have found that often children have better insights on these hard life questions than the adults!

I lost my dad.

No, not in the grocery store,

or on the second floor of a big department store.

No, not around the block,

or under a rock,

or in a drawer with all the socks.

I lost my dad. He was a tall, thin man with a big, red beard,

and a heart as full as the hair on his chin.

I lost my dad.
He died from an awful disease--

One that doesn't care about how much I loved him,

or how much he loved me.

I lost my dad a long time ago, but I found that my dad is very much around--

not on the street, but more in the kindness of people I meet.

I found my dad not far from home.

I'm all grown up
and have a big bushy beard like my dad.
And now, like my dad--I have a son.

One who loves me

as much as I love him.

I found my dad in the two of us.

Mom, Dad, and Fen have fun at the zoo

Lauren Persons:
Author of *Lost But Found*, teacher, writer, and devoted grandmother

Noah Hrbek:
Illustrator of *Lost But Found*, artist, actor, musician, and loving father

Add YOUR special memories here

About the Author — Lauren E. Persons

As the story goes, I didn't start talking until I was two and then--never stopped. With an English teacher for a mother, words became my wallpaper. As the middle kid in a loud household, I figured out the only way to get my voice heard—be dramatic! While many chil-dren have endearing nicknames, my family dubbed me Sarah Berhardt, the famous melodramatic, French actress. Little did I know that my passion for words and drama would collide and serve me well as an English and drama teacher, theatre director, actress, poet and playwright.

About the Illustrator — Noah Hrbek

Before I could even walk or talk, I wanted to ex-press myself through art. That interest has grown ex-ponentially through the years, and continues to lead me to a wide variety of artistic opportunities and ex-periences. This has included the theater arts, music, video, painting, sculpting, graphic design, and more recently, illustration. Creating drawings for this book has been a project that is particularly close to my heart, not only because I myself am a father, but be-cause Lauren's son has been my closest friend, quite literally, since he and I were both infants.

CPSIA information can be obtained
at www.ICGtesting.com
Printed in the USA
BVHW021447091220
595275BV00009B/270